TRICKY

For Jaxon and Brooklyn

Thanks to Lisa Cinar and Cynthia Nugent for their indispensable feedback.

Text and Illustrations © Kari Rust 2017

Owlkids Books acknowledges the financial support of the Canada Council for the Arts, the Ontario Arts Council, the Government of Canada through the Canada Book Fund (CBF) and the Government of Ontario through the Ontario Media Development Corporation's Book Initiative for our publishing activities.

Published in Canada by
Owlkids Books Inc.
10 Lower Spadina Avenue
Toronto, ON M5V 2Z2

Published in the United States by
Owlkids Books Inc.
1700 Fourth Street
Berkeley, CA 94710

Library and Archives Canada Cataloguing in Publication

Rust, Kari, author, illustrator
     Tricky / written and illustrated by Kari Rust.

ISBN 978-1-77147-252-4 (hardcover)

     I. Title.

PS8635.U883T75 2017   jC813'.6   C2017-900011-X

Library of Congress Control Number: 2016962523

The art in this book was created with a mix of traditional media composited and coloured in Photoshop.
The text is set in New Century Schoolbook.
Edited by: Debbie Rogosin
Designed by: Claudia Dávila

ONTARIO ARTS COUNCIL
CONSEIL DES ARTS DE L'ONTARIO
an Ontario government agency
un organisme du gouvernement de l'Ontario

Canada Council
for the Arts

Conseil des Arts
du Canada

Canadä

Manufactured in Shenzhen, Guangdong, China, in April 2017, by WKT Co. Ltd.
Job #16CB3153

A   B   C   D   E   F

 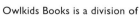 

Publisher of Chirp, chickaDEE and OWL
www.owlkidsbooks.com | Owlkids Books is a division of   Bayard
CANADA

TRICKY

Kari Rust

Owlkids Books

The Duke and Tricky were well-known in their town.

Known for cheating and thievery.

Known for being greedy and mean.

Known for playing cruel jokes on the townspeople, just for fun. The Duke knew every trick in the book, and he had taught them all to Tricky.

After dinner each night, over some hot tea, the Duke would whoop and laugh about the day's mischief while Tricky snuffled and rolled on the rug.

Then they'd shuffle off to bed
for a good night's sleep.

One morning, when they went for their usual breakfast at the bakery, the Duke and Tricky were surprised to find a new baker working there. Ms. Paisley had just moved to town.

The Duke was always delighted to meet newcomers.

When the Duke stepped out for his newspaper, Ms. Paisley gave Tricky a friendly pat and a wonderful treat.

That evening, Tricky thought about Ms. Paisley.

He had never been given a treat like that
before, and it made him feel warm inside.

The following day, the Duke
saw a chance for mischief.

And for the first time, Tricky realized
that what they were doing was WRONG.

As they left the bakery, the warm feeling he had about
Ms. Paisley turned into fiery red anger toward the Duke.
Tricky had to do something! But what?

All he knew was TRICKS.

When they got home, Tricky played
his first trick on the Duke.

The loaf of bread made a grumpy
gurgle as he flushed it down.

He played another trick...

and another...

This went on and on, until at last, the Duke figured it out.

The Duke was FURIOUS! No one had ever played a trick on *him* before. He threw Tricky out of the house and slammed the door.

Cold and wet, Tricky wandered alone into the night.

When Ms. Paisley arrived at the bakery early in the morning, there was Tricky. He spent the day watching her work. No tricks. No cheats.

When the bakery closed, Tricky followed Ms. Paisley home.

And there he stayed.

The Duke carried on making mischief without Tricky...

...but it wasn't the same.

It turned out that he missed his old dog more than he expected.
So, one dark night, the Duke packed up and left town.

They say that you can't teach an old dog
new tricks. But Tricky *did* learn new tricks…

...good ones!

And if old dogs can learn new tricks, perhaps the Duke could too.